PLEASANT COMPANY ®

PRESENTS

THE AMERICAN GIRLS
COLLECTION®

18 · 54

MEET KIRSTEN · An American Girl
KIRSTEN LEARNS A LESSON · A School Story
KIRSTEN'S SURPRISE · A Christmas Story
HAPPY BIRTHDAY, KIRSTEN! · A Springtime Story
KIRSTEN SAVES THE DAY · A Summer Story
CHANGES FOR KIRSTEN · A Winter Story

19 · 04

MEET SAMANTHA · An American Girl
SAMANTHA LEARNS A LESSON · A School Story
SAMANTHA'S SURPRISE · A Christmas Story
HAPPY BIRTHDAY, SAMANTHA! · A Springtime Story
SAMANTHA SAVES THE DAY · A Summer Story
CHANGES FOR SAMANTHA · A Winter Story

19 · 44

MEET MOLLY · An American (
MOLLY LEARNS A LESSON · A Scho(
MOLLY'S SURPRISE · A Christmas
HAPPY BIRTHDAY, MOLLY! · A Springti(
MOLLY SAVES THE DAY · A Summer Story
CHANGES FOR MOLLY · A Winter Story

MOLLY
SAVES
THE DAY
A SUMMER STORY

BY VALERIE TRIPP

ILLUSTRATIONS NICK BACKES

VIGNETTES KEITH SKEEN

SCHOLASTIC INC.

NEW YORK   TORONTO   LONDON   AUCKLAND   SYDNEY

PICTURE CREDITS

The following individuals and organizations have generously given permission to reprint illustrations contained in "Looking Back": pp. 64-65—Printed by permission of the Estate of Norman Rockwell, Copyright © 1940 Estate of Norman Rockwell; State Historical Society of Wisconsin; Courtesy Chrysler Corporation; Camp Counseling, Fourth Edition, A. Viola Mitchell, et. al., Philadelphia: W.B. Saunders Company, 1970; pp. 66-67—Photograph by Barbara Morgan; Courtesy of the Girl Scouts of the U.S.A.; Camp Counseling, Fourth Edition, A. Viola Mitchell, et. al., Philadelphia: W.B. Saunders Company, 1970; Courtesy of the Girl Scouts of the U.S.A.; Courtesy of the American Red Cross; Photograph by Barbara Morgan; pp. 68-69—Courtesy of the Girl Scouts of the U.S.A.; Photograph by Barbara Morgan; Courtesy of the Girl Scouts of the U.S.A.; Camp Counseling, Fourth Edition, A. Viola Mitchell, et. al., Philadelphia: W.B. Saunders Company, 1970.

Edited by Jeanne Thieme
Designed by Myland McRevey
Art Directed by Kathleen A. Brown

ISBN 0-590-45080-8

12 11 10 9 8 7   4 5 6 7/9

Printed in the U.S.A.   23

First Scholastic printing, January 1992

TO PLEASANT

TABLE OF CONTENTS

MOLLY'S FAMILY

MOLLY
A ten-year-old who is growing up on the home front in America during World War Two.

DAD
Molly's father, a doctor who is somewhere in England, taking care of wounded soldiers.

MOM
Molly's mother, who holds the family together while Dad is away.

JILL
Molly's fifteen-year-old sister, who is always trying to act grown-up.

RICKY

*Molly's thirteen-year-old
brother—a big pest.*

BRAD

*Molly's six-year-old
brother—a little pest.*

MRS. GILFORD

*The housekeeper,
who rules the roost when
Mom is at work.*

LINDA

*One of Molly's best
friends, a practical
schemer.*

SUSAN

*Molly's other best
friend, a cheerful
dreamer.*

CAMP
GOWONAGIN

Molly McIntire loved Camp Gowonagin from the very first day she was there.

Molly and her friends Linda and Susan had never gone to summer camp before. They were a little nervous when the big old bus that brought them from home stopped inside the camp's gate. But as soon as they stepped off the bus with all the other campers, they were met by cheering Camp Gowonagin counselors. The counselors sang to them:

> "Welcome to Camp Gowonagin!
> We're mighty glad you're here!
> Hurray! Hurrah! for Gowonagin!
> Hail! Hail! Let's give a cheer!"

"Gosh!" said Susan. "This is neat!"

Molly just grinned happily.

A roly-poly woman came toward them. She was beaming. "Hello, girls!" she said. "My name is Miss Butternut. I'm the camp director. Welcome to Camp Gowonagin! The counselors and I are very happy you're here."

"Hurray!" cheered the counselors.

Miss Butternut laughed. "You see?" she said to the campers. "We're going to have a wonderful time. Now, if you'll follow me, I'll show you to your tents."

The campers gathered their suitcases and duffel bags and followed Miss Butternut up the shady path. There were big brown tents on one side of the path. On the other side, Molly saw wide green fields edged with darker green pine trees. The open fields sloped down to a silver-blue lake with an island in the middle. "It's beautiful here," Molly said.

"Yes," said Linda. "There's so much *sky*."

Miss Butternut led Molly, Linda, and Susan to Tent Number Six, where they would live with five

2

other girls. As they carried their gear into the roomy tent, Miss Butternut smiled and said, "Here you are! This is your home sweet home for the next two weeks. Remember our Camp Gowonagin motto, 'Tidy and True.' Keep your tent neat and clean. Then you will be comfortable and happy at Camp Gowonagin."

Molly *was* comfortable and happy at camp right away. The counselors were so nice and friendly, they made everything fun and easy. Molly, Linda, and Susan soon made friends with the girls in their tent and lots of the other campers. "Old campers"— girls who had been at camp last summer—taught them the camp songs and cheers. Molly liked the cheer that went

"Gowonagin! Gowonagin!
Go on again and try! (Clap, clap)
You can win! You can win!
Go on again and try! (Clap, clap)"

In just a few days, Molly felt like one of the old campers herself. She knew all the rules and the way everything was done at Camp Gowonagin. She and Linda and Susan kept their tent and their belongings in order. Even Linda, who was messy at home, tried to live up to the "Tidy" part of the camp motto. She always tied her camp tie and kept her shirt tucked in, just like the counselors did.

There was something for everyone at Camp Gowonagin. Linda liked using the bows and arrows in archery. Susan liked campfires, sing alongs, and wienie roasts. Molly liked nature hikes, when Miss Butternut taught them the names of the plants and trees and birds. Every day the girls learned something new. Every day was so busy and so much fun, the time just flew by.

Days at camp began early. Miss Butternut stood by the flagpole and blew a cheerful tune on her bugle. The words to the tune were

"I can't get 'em up, I can't get 'em up,
I can't get 'em up in the morning!"

But in Molly's case, the words were wrong. She couldn't wait to get up in the morning and begin the day. There was so much to do! First there was Morning Flag Raising Ceremony and breakfast in the Dining Hall. Then the campers played games of softball, volleyball, and basketball. They had lessons in swimming, tennis, and sailing. On rainy days, they worked on their arts and crafts projects.

Susan was making a leaf and bark chart. Molly was making a sit-upon. She folded a piece of oilcloth around an old newspaper and sewed the edges together. Linda was braiding strings together to make a lanyard—a cord to hang a whistle on and wear around her neck. All the counselors had lanyards. Linda noticed everything about the counselors.

One of Molly's favorite times at camp was Evening Flag Lowering Ceremony. She liked it because all the girls and all the counselors stood together and sang the Camp Gowonagin song:

"God bless Gowonagin!
Camp that we love!
Raise the flag high,
Never say die,
While the red, white, and blue
    flies above!"

Molly always got goose bumps up and down her arms when they sang the camp song. Standing shoulder to shoulder with all the other campers made her feel proud. She *did* love Camp Gowon-agin. She was glad to be there with her two best friends.

*Molly always got goose bumps up and down her arms
when they sang the camp song.*

One evening, after the flag was lowered and folded, Miss Butternut said, "Before we go up to dinner, I'm pleased to tell you the winner of the Camp Gowonagin canoe race. First place goes to Dorinda Brassy. Let's have a cheer for Dorinda."

All the campers cheered, "Hip, hip hurray! Hip, hip hurray!"

Dorinda looked smug as everyone cheered. She was an old camper, and she was used to winning.

Miss Butternut went on in her kindly way, "And what do we say to the new camper who came in last?"

All the campers cheered:

"Gowonagin! Gowonagin!
Go on again and try!
You can win! You can win!
Go on again and try!"

Miss Butternut nodded happily. "That's the spirit!" she said. "Here at Camp Gowonagin, we know that trying is as important as winning." She smiled. "All right, girls! I'll see you in the Dining Hall in two minutes."

"Go on again and try," repeated Susan as the girls walked up to the Dining Hall. "I *do* try. I just

7

can not get my canoe to go straight." Susan was the camper who came in last in the canoe race. "No matter what I do, my paddle won't work right," she sighed.

"Well," said Linda glumly, "don't worry. Pretty soon we'll be home where there's no place to paddle except the bathtub. We have only three more days here." She looked around sadly. "I'm going to miss camp."

"Oh, me too," said Susan. "I'm going to miss absolutely everything at camp except canoeing." She looked at Molly. "You probably feel exactly the way I do, Molly. You're going to miss everything at camp except swimming underwater, right? You hate that the way I hate canoeing."

Molly didn't say anything. She was a little embarrassed. She wished Susan wouldn't compare her poor canoeing with Molly's swimming. "I don't hate swimming," Molly said a little crossly. "I just don't like being underwater. But you don't have to blab it all over the place."

"*I'm* not blabbing it," said Susan. "Everybody in the whole camp knows you won't jump in the water or even get your head wet. We all saw you fall off the dock and almost drown that time."

"Yeah," said Linda. "We saw the counselors save your life. Remember how they jumped right in and pulled you out?"

Molly certainly *did* remember. She would never forget the day she slipped off the dock and fell into the deep water. The dark, dense green water closed over her head. She couldn't see, or breathe, or move. Though she was only under the water for a few seconds, it seemed like a long, long time to Molly. After the counselors pulled her out, Miss  Butternut sat next to her, holding her wet bathing cap, until Molly caught her breath. "Don't you worry," Miss Butternut said. "You'll swim underwater when you're good and ready."

But camp was almost over. And Molly was no closer to swimming underwater than ever.

"Look at it this way," Susan said cheerfully as they sat at their table in the Dining Hall. "You and I will just have to come back to camp next summer, so we can—"

"Go on again and try!" Molly and Linda chimed in. And Molly had to laugh.

9

Just as they finished dinner, Miss Butternut stood up and said, "Tonight, girls, I have a special announcement to make." She rose up on her toes, as if the good news was trying to spill out by itself. When everyone was quiet, she went on. "One of our favorite traditions here at Camp Gowonagin is our game of Color War."

Whistles and cheers rang out through the Dining Hall. Miss Butternut smiled. "I can see the old campers remember how much fun Color War is! I know the new campers will love it, too. Now, when we play Color War, the whole camp is divided into two teams: the Reds and the Blues. The team lists are on the doors. You may see which team you are on as you leave."

Everyone quickly swung around to look at the doors, as if something as exciting as the lists might shoot off sparks. But the doors looked as quiet as usual.

"Tomorrow morning," said Miss Butternut, "the Red Team will paddle canoes across the narrow part of the lake to Chocolate Drop Island. They'll put the flag at the top of the hill there. It will be the Red Team's job to guard the flag. The Blue Team will have its headquarters here at camp, at the boathouse. They'll try to figure out a way to capture the flag from the Reds. The team that has the flag at sundown wins the game."

Miss Butternut went on. "When the Blues try to capture the flag, they have to be very fast and very smart, or the Red Team will catch them and put them in prison. Prisoners can be freed only if someone from their own team tags them without being caught by the prison guard." Miss Butternut's eyes twinkled. "One last thing," she said. "The counselors and I will be watching you to be sure everyone is safe. But we'll be well hidden, so you probably won't see us." The counselors smiled and nodded. "Any questions?" asked Miss Butternut.

Dorinda Brassy raised her hand. "When will we choose the leaders?" she asked.

"Both teams will meet after dinner to elect their captains," said Miss Butternut. "Anyone may be elected."

"Just look at Dorinda," whispered Linda. "She's *so* sure she's going to be a leader."

Molly looked. Linda was right. Dorinda and her

friend Patty already seemed to be taking command. Molly envied them. It would be neat to be in charge. Molly pictured herself leading a team to victory. Her team would capture the flag and canoe back to camp, with everyone cheering and clapping and singing the camp song. . . .

"Off you go!" said Miss Butternut.

Molly was practically knocked off her chair by campers charging to see the team lists. By the time Molly got to the doors, she was too far back in the crowd to see anything. But Linda elbowed her way through the crowd to the front, then elbowed her way back to report to Molly and Susan.

"You two are Blues," she said. "I'm a Red."

"Does that mean we're enemies?" asked Susan.

"Not until tomorrow," said Linda with a grin. "I've got to go now. The Red Team is meeting in Tent Number Four to elect a leader. I bet you my bug repellent it'll be Patty. See you later!" She waved as the Reds swarmed out the door.

Later that night, when all the campers were settled in their cots, they heard Miss Butternut play

"Taps" on her bugle. That was the signal for lights out.

Molly listened to the bugle's gentle song. All the girls in the tent sang along softly:

"Day is done.
Gone the sun,
From the lake, from the hills,
    from the sky.
All is well. Safely rest. God is nigh."

Usually, Molly drifted off to sleep peacefully, wondering what wonderful new activity the next day would bring. But tonight she was too wound up. She turned on her flashlight, rolled over on her side, and whispered to Linda and Susan, "Are you asleep?"

"Nope," said Susan.

"Neither am I," said Linda. "What's the matter?"

"I've been thinking," said Molly. "I'm not sure I like the idea of Color War."

"Me either," said Susan.

"How come?" asked Linda. She flopped over onto her stomach and propped her chin on her pillow.

"Well, in the first place, how do we know what

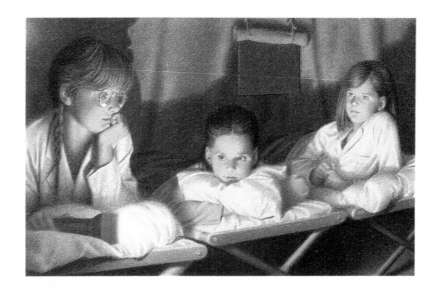

to do?" asked Molly. "I've never been in a Color War before."

"Listen," said Linda. "Isn't little Miss First Place Dorinda the captain of your team? You can bet she will tell you and all the rest of the Blues exactly what to do."

"That's just it," said Molly. "The game sounded like fun when Miss Butternut explained it at dinner. But you should have seen Dorinda at our team's meeting. As soon as she was chosen captain, she started calling us the Blue Army. And she was so serious! She acted like the *general* of a real army."

"Molly's right," Susan agreed. "Dorinda's awfully bossy."

"Yeah," said Molly. "And what if she tells me to do something terrible, like . . ."

"Like dive in over your head and swim underwater?" Linda finished for her. "If Dorinda tells you to dive, tell her to go jump in the lake. Get it?"

"It's not a joke, Linda," said Molly. "Dorinda's in charge now. I have to do what she says."

"Yes," said Susan. "We're in Dorinda's army now. We have to follow her orders. Everything is different."

"I liked the way camp was before," said Molly. "I don't see why we have to mess everything up and go capturing flags."

"Especially in canoes," added Susan.

Linda shook her head. "It's just a game. It's supposed to be fun, not something to worry about. I mean, if we were going off to a real war or something, then I could see being worried and scared."

Molly nodded. "My dad told us he was scared before he went away to war," she said. "But he said it was okay to be scared because that meant he had a chance to be brave."

"Well, maybe this Color War will give us a chance to be brave," said Linda. "If you can do something you're scared to do, then you're brave."

"That's easy for you to say," said Susan. "You're not scared of canoeing like I am or swimming underwater like Molly is."

"Yeah," said Molly, "you're not scared of anything."

"Oh, yes I am," said Linda.

"Like what?" asked Susan.

"Well," said Linda, "it's really stupid but I'm scared of creepy crawly things, like spiders and bugs. Worms are the worst." Linda moved her fingers like wiggling worms and made a face so that Molly and Susan had to laugh. "Slimy worms! Ugh! I hate them!"

"Really?" said Molly. It cheered her up to know that Linda was scared of something sort of silly, like worms.

"Yes, really," said Linda. "But at least I can joke about it. You don't see me lying awake at night worrying about it. So don't you two worry

16

about Dorinda, or canoes, or swimming underwater. Don't take this Color War so seriously. It won't last forever, right?"

"Right," said Molly and Susan.

"Okay," said Linda. She rolled over and pulled her blankets up to her chin. "Go to sleep and that's an order!"

"Yes sir!" giggled Susan. She rolled over and closed her eyes.

Molly turned off her flashlight and closed her eyes, but she didn't follow the order. She didn't fall asleep for a long, long time. Linda wasn't worried about the Color War, but Molly still was. Maybe the Color War would be her big chance to be brave. But she wondered if she really wanted that chance.

WE'RE IN THE ARMY NOW

The next morning, every camper put on a red armband or a blue armband to show which team she was on. Right after breakfast, the Red Team left the Dining Hall with the flag. Molly and Susan watched Linda march down the path toward the Red canoes with the rest of her team. They looked like an army, parading two by two like soldiers, carrying their bag lunches, and singing:

"We are the Reds,
Mighty, mighty Reds.
Everywhere we go-oh,
People want to know-oh,
Who we are.

So we tell them:
We are the Reds,
Mighty, mighty Reds . . .''

Linda turned around and rolled her eyes at Molly. Molly grinned. She remembered what Linda had said last night about not taking Color War too seriously. *I should be more like Linda,* Molly thought. But she snapped to attention when Dorinda said in her bossiest voice, ''Blue Army report to HQ on the double.''

''HQ?'' Susan asked Molly. ''Who's that?''

''It's not a person, it's a place,'' said Molly. ''HQ stands for headquarters. I think she means the boathouse. Let's go.''

Molly and Susan followed the rest of the Blue Army to the boathouse. Two girls stood as guards at the door in case the Red Army had left spies behind. When she got the signal that the coast was clear, Dorinda began.

She frowned at the girls. ''*We* are going to win this Color War,'' she said sternly. ''And the only way to win is to fight as hard as we can. Do you understand?''

Everyone mumbled, ''Yes.''

19

"All right," Dorinda went on. "Here is the plan of attack. The flag is on Chocolate Drop Island. To get it, we obviously have to canoe across the lake. You will each be assigned a buddy. You and your buddy will paddle a canoe together. We will load up and begin the attack at oh-nine-hundred."

"Oh-nine-hundred?" Susan whispered to Molly. "Where's that?"

"It's not a place, it's a time," said Molly. "It's the army way to say nine o'clock."

"Well, why doesn't she just say nine o'clock?" asked Susan. "We're a team. We're not *really* an army."

Molly put a finger to her lips. Dorinda was scowling at her and at Susan.

"Pay attention, troops!" Dorinda ordered. She turned and uncovered a big map of Camp Gowonagin tacked to the wall.

Everyone said, "Oooh." The map looked as if it had been very carefully drawn. Molly realized Dorinda and her helpers must have been up all night making it. Molly's heart sank. Under

20

Dorinda's command, Color War seemed less and less like a game among friends and more and more like a war between enemies.

The map showed the boathouse, the lake, and Chocolate Drop Island. Dorinda used a long stick to point to places on the map as she talked.

First, she pointed to the boathouse. "We will set out from here," she said. Then she pointed to a place on the far side of Chocolate Drop Island labeled "BEACH." "We will land here. From the beach we will march up Chocolate Drop Hill. *I* will capture the flag. The rest of you will take the Red Army prisoner. You will lead the prisoners back to your canoes and return them to our HQ. I will meet you here no later than ten-hundred."

"She means ten o'clock, right?" Susan asked Molly.

But Molly wasn't listening to Susan. There was something she didn't understand. It wasn't the plan. She understood the plan perfectly. The plan was easy. In fact, it was too easy, much too easy. Timidly, Molly raised her hand. Everyone turned around and stared at her.

"Yes?" snapped Dorinda.

Molly stood up. She clasped her hands behind her back. "Uh, I get the plan," she said. "I know what we're supposed to do. But I wonder what they're going to do. The Red Army, I mean. Won't they have scouts who will see us coming across the lake? The lake isn't very wide there."

"How do *you* think we should cross the lake?" Dorinda asked sharply. "Should we swim underwater?"

Molly's hands were clammy. Everyone at camp knew she hated to swim underwater. She wanted to sit down, but she made herself speak up. "I just think the Red Army will be waiting for us at the beach when we land. They'll be ready to take all of us prisoner. Isn't there any place we could land where they wouldn't see us?"

"No," said Dorinda. "Those are my orders."

"But," Molly started to say, "but what if—"

Dorinda crossed her arms over her chest and said, "If you are too chicken to do this you can stay behind. Be a deserter. Otherwise, go with your friend Susan. The two of you can be buddies and bring up the rear in your canoe. That way the rest

"How do you think we should cross the lake?"
Dorinda asked sharply. "Should we swim underwater?"

of us can protect you."

Molly sat down, shamed into quiet. She pretended to straighten her blue armband.

"Now, go to the canoes! The rest of the buddy assignments will be made there," said Dorinda. Everyone filed out of the boathouse. No one would look at Molly.

Susan and Molly walked slowly over to the last canoe on the shore. "How come we don't get lunches like the Red Army did?" asked Susan. "Won't we get hungry?"

"We shouldn't need lunches," said Molly. "We're supposed to be back here by ten o'clock, remember?"

"Oh yeah," said Susan. She looked longingly toward the Dining Hall.

"Head out!" they heard Dorinda yell. All the Blues cheered and waved their canoe paddles in the air. Molly pushed the canoe into the water. She started to climb in the back.

"Wait!" said Susan. "I don't want to sit in the front. I'll get splashed by waves up there."

Molly looked at the water. It was as flat as glass. But she said, "Okay, you can sit in the back."

Susan looked uncertain. "Nooo," she said. "I don't want to sit in the back, either. The back person does all the work. You know how bad I am at steering and everything."

"Hurry and make up your mind," said Molly. "The other canoes are already halfway to the island."

"Okay, okay," said Susan. "I'll go in the front. But don't paddle too fast." The canoe wobbled from side to side as Susan climbed in. "See?" she squeaked. "I always get the tippiest canoe." She inched her way to the seat in front, clutching the sides of the canoe with both hands. When she was seated, Molly handed her a paddle, shoved the canoe into deeper water, and climbed in the back. The other canoes were way ahead of them, strung out across the lake like a family of ducks.

As she and Susan paddled closer to the island, Molly could see the Red scout watching them from a high point on the island's shore. The scout turned and ran toward the back side of the island. *She's going to the beach to warn everyone,* Molly thought with a sinking feeling. *The whole and entire Red*

Army will be waiting for us at the beach. They are going to put us in prison. I just know it.

The rest of the Blue canoes had already paddled around to the back side of the island, out of Molly's sight. "Come on," she said to Susan. "We'd better catch up with the others." She dug her paddle deep into the water.

Susan dug her paddle in, too. Then she shrieked, "My paddle! I dropped it!"

Molly saw Susan's paddle floating toward her. She put her own paddle in the bottom of the canoe and reached out with both hands to grab Susan's paddle. Susan was reaching, too, leaning way out over the side of the canoe.

"Don't!" yelled Molly. But it was too late. Over went Susan. Over went the canoe. Over went Molly. Down, down into the water Molly sank, down into the dark green depths. Molly struggled with all her strength, pulling with one arm, grabbing on to her glasses with the other hand, kicking with her legs, wiggling and fighting her way up. Finally, her head popped out into the sunshine. Molly coughed and choked on the water she had swallowed. She gasped for air.

26

"Over here!" Molly heard Susan shout. She looked around. Susan was behind her, holding on to the canoe. "Come on!" Susan said. "Grab the canoe!"

Molly swam toward Susan. She held her head up high out of the water. It felt odd, swimming in her clothes. Her shoes felt like weights, dragging her feet down. Molly kicked hard. The canoe was right side up, but it was half full of water. Her paddle floated inside in a big puddle. Molly held on to the canoe and tried to catch her breath.

"I'm so sorry," Susan wailed. "Are you okay? What'll we do?"

"Go to shore," said Molly in a shaky voice. "I think I see a place to land."

They were not far from the island. Both girls held on to the canoe with one arm and pushed through the water with the other arm. As they came to the shore, Molly saw a place where the water cut into the land. She and Susan pushed the canoe into the cut. It was narrow, not much wider than the canoe. They scrambled out of the water and sat on the rocks, panting.

Molly was still trembling.

"Gosh," Susan whispered, "I hope the Red Team doesn't catch us."

Molly looked around. They were completely hidden by a high wall of rocky land on one side and tall pine trees on the other. "I don't think anyone can see us here," she said. "The scout is on the other side of those trees, and I think the rest of them are on the far side of the island, on the beach. Probably no one knows about this little place to land. But we'd better not stay long. Let's bail out the canoe."

Molly and Susan scooped water out of the canoe with their Camp Gowonagin hats. When there was still about three inches of water sloshing around the bottom of the canoe, Susan said, "My arms are killing me. Can't we stop now?"

"Okay," said Molly. Her arms hurt, too. "Let's go."

"Good," said Susan. "I'm so hungry. And I want to change my clothes."

"Oh, we can't go back to camp," said Molly firmly. "We have to go on and find the rest of our army."

Susan protested, "But it's nearly lunchtime! And I lost my paddle!"

"I'll paddle," said Molly. She stood up.

Wearily, Susan climbed back into the canoe. "We're probably better off if I don't have a paddle," she said. "We sure can't do any worse."

Molly backed the canoe into the lake by pushing against the rocks with her paddle. Then, slowly, she paddled around the corner of the island until they could see the beach.

"Uh oh," said Susan.

All the Blue canoes were dragged out of the water on one side of the beach. Paddles stuck out every which way. The canoes looked as helpless as tipped-over turtles waving their legs in the air.

All the girls in the Blue Army were sitting behind the canoes in a bushy corner of the beach. A big sign on one bush said "PRISON."

"Look at that!" said Susan. "They've got our whole team in their prison, exactly like you said they would."

Standing in front of the prison was a watchful guard with a big whistle on a lanyard around her neck. Molly squinted at the guard through her water-stained glasses. She gasped, "It's Linda! The guard is Linda!" Molly was surprised. She certainly had not expected Linda to have such an important job to do.

"Oh, good," said Susan, relieved. "She can help us." Susan waved her arms above her head. "Yoo-hoo! Linda! It's us!" she shouted. "Help!"

"Susan, I don't know if . . ." Molly began.

At that second, Linda looked straight at Susan and Molly. She put her whistle in her mouth and blew one shrill blast after another. She ran down to the water, swooping toward them like a hawk in attack, waving her arms wildly and pointing to their canoe. Five or six girls with red armbands ran across the beach toward her.

"They'll catch us!" cried Molly. "Let's get out of here!" She paddled hard. Susan stuck her arms in the water and used her hands as paddles. Luckily, the canoe was pretty far out in the lake, and it scooted around to the other side of the island before the Red canoes were even in the water. But Molly didn't stop paddling as hard as she could until she and Susan were all the way across the

Linda swooped toward them like a hawk in attack.
"Let's get out of here!" cried Molly.

lake, safe at the boathouse.

Silently, Molly and Susan hauled their canoe out of the water. It was the only canoe on the shore, the last Blue canoe that was free, and it looked lonely. Molly's shoulders were sore. Her hands hurt from gripping the paddle.

Susan shook her head. "I just can't believe Linda would send them out to get us like that," she said. "We're her friends."

"I know," said Molly. "And Linda told us she wasn't going to take Color War too seriously."

"She must have changed her mind," said Susan. "She sure looked serious back there."

"Yeah," said Molly. "She's as serious as Dorinda." Molly felt as if Linda had tricked her in some way. Last night, Linda had said this war would be fun. So far, it had not been very much fun for Molly, that was for sure. *First, I practically drown,* she thought. *Then, even worse, my best friend treats me like an enemy. I guess friendship doesn't count during a war.*

Molly and Susan trudged up the hill to their tent. Molly was thinking hard. "After we change clothes, maybe we can dig up some lunch," said

Susan. She sounded cheerful.

"First we'd better dig up a plan," said Molly. She sounded serious.

CREEPY CRAWLIES

"They don't have to be real worms. She just has to think they're worms," said Molly. She and Susan were crawling in the dirt under the wooden platform beneath their tent. They were digging with the cups from their mess kits to find worms. "We can use bugs and spiders, too. I saw lots of them under here last week during Camp Clean-up. And get sticks and stems like this, see?" Molly held up a stem. It was brown and slimy enough to look like a worm.

"Ugh!" squirmed Susan. "I don't like this plan. I think it's mean."

Molly sighed. "Do you have another idea?" she asked.

"No," said Susan, "but I don't see why we have to do something so mean to Linda. She's our best friend."

"We're not doing it to Linda," said Molly. "We're doing it to the Red Army. You can't think of people as people during a war. You think of them as part of an army."

"Well . . ." Susan began.

"Look," said Molly sharply. "Linda sure wasn't thinking of us as her friends when she blew the whistle on us, was she?"

"No," admitted Susan.

"So we shouldn't think of her as our friend Linda. We should think of her as the guard for the Red Army. She's got *our* whole army in her prison. We have to get them free or we won't even have a chance to capture the flag and win the Color War. That's why we have to do this," said Molly.

"This" was Molly's plan. It depended on worms. Molly and Susan grubbed in the dirt on their hands and knees. Molly's shirt stuck to her back. Susan's face was red and sweaty.

"I've sweated so much I'm wetter than I was when I fell in the lake," complained Susan.

"Well, we'd better stop," said Molly. Her hands were grimy.

Susan held up an old tin can. It was only half full of worms and bugs and stems. "There's not very much stuff in here," she said.

"There's not very much *time*," said Molly. "We'll have to go now."

"Okay," said Susan. She and Molly wiggled like worms themselves to get out from under the tent. The sky was white hot as they plodded back to the boathouse.

Molly pushed the canoe into the water. She started to get in the back.

Susan said, "No sir! I'm not getting in the front again. That's the tippiest part."

"No it isn't," said Molly.

But Susan was stubborn. "I'm NOT getting in the front of that canoe again and that's final. Do you want to tip over like the last time?"

Molly remembered her plunge into the water. "All right," she said. "I'll get in the front. But I won't be able to help you paddle. The Red scout has got to think there's only one of us in the canoe or she might guess the plan."

"Well, you lie down," said Susan. "The scout won't be able to see you."

So Molly laid down on the bottom of the canoe next to the extra paddle, and Susan pushed off. With Susan paddling, the canoe jerked forward like a darting fish. It rolled from side to side, but it did move. Soon Susan said, "There's the Red scout. She sees me."

"Just keep paddling," hissed Molly. They were not far from the island. The canoe zigzagged, sometimes heading away from the island, then heading straight for it.

"Susan," said Molly, "you're supposed to switch your paddle from side to side every few strokes so the canoe will go in a line."

"I can't do it that way," said Susan shortly. "I'm doing it the only way I know how."

"Maybe that's good," said Molly. "It will confuse the Red scout. She won't be able to figure out what you're trying to do. Now, head for that hidden landing place we found last time."

In a surprisingly short time, they got to the landing place they'd found when the canoe tipped over. Susan banged the canoe on the rocks, but she managed to get it into the narrow space.

Molly sat up. "Okay," she said. "Give me your paddle. Here are the worms." The plan was for Molly to paddle the canoe around to the beach. Susan would climb around the edge of the island to the prison and free the rest of the Blue Army. Then she would swim out to Molly and the canoe.

But Susan held on to the paddle. "Listen," she said, "the Red scout just saw me paddling across the lake. Won't she think it's funny if she sees you paddle around to the beach? I think I should stay with the canoe and you should do the worm and prisoner part."

"But that means you'll have to handle the canoe all by yourself," said Molly. "Are you sure you can do it?"

Susan shrugged. "I don't know," she said. "I got us this far, maybe I can do the rest. Anyway, I'll try."

Molly looked at Susan. "You're pretty brave," she said.

"You've got the hard part," said Susan. "You might get caught by the Red Army."

"No," said Molly with a little grin. "I figure they will be so busy watching the way you paddle a canoe, they'll never notice me."

Susan smiled. "Good luck," she said. As Molly scrambled up the rocks, Susan backed the canoe into the lake.

Molly moved as quickly as she could, staying very close to the water. For a while she could see Susan's canoe moving along offshore. Then the canoe disappeared around a point of land and Molly couldn't see it anymore.

Molly crept around the shore toward the prison. She kept a sharp lookout for the Red Army. Suddenly, Molly stopped. Here was a surprise. The path was gone! She was standing at the edge of an inlet that cut into the shore of Chocolate Drop Island. Molly could see the prison on the other side of the inlet. *Why wasn't this inlet on Dorinda's map?* Molly asked herself. The water looked deep. *Well,* thought Molly, *I'll just have to swim across to get to the prison. There's no other way.*

She put the can of worms down her undershirt and tucked her shirt tightly into her shorts. Then

39

she waded into the water. When it reached her
shoulders, Molly dog paddled as quietly as she
could, keeping her head well above the water.
When she was about halfway across, she stopped.
Oh, no! she thought. *Linda!* Linda was walking
through the bushes behind the prison. She was
coming right toward Molly. Linda's whistle glinted
in the sun.

Molly held her breath, as if that would make
her invisible. *If Linda sees me, I'm done for,* she
thought. *The whole Blue Army is done for!* But there
was no place to hide in the middle of the water.
There was nowhere to go but . . .

Down, thought Molly. *I'll have to swim
underwater.* Molly shuddered. *I can't make myself do
it,* she thought. But Linda was coming closer and
closer and closer. . . . Quickly, Molly took a deep
breath and slid down under the surface.

The water swallowed her. She forced herself to
open her eyes. Greeny gold sunlight filtered
through the water. Plants writhed like snakes next
to her. *Maybe if I move it won't be so bad,* Molly
thought. She fluttered her legs and pulled with her
arms. The can of worms was cold against her skin.

Finally, she couldn't hold her breath any longer. She bobbed up for air. Thank goodness! Linda had turned her back. She was moving away from Molly, watching something out in the big lake off the opposite end of the beach. It was Susan, waving her paddle around, slapping it against the water, calling, "Yoo-hoo! Yoo-hoo!"

The Red Army girls were all watching Susan. They buzzed like confused bees. "Get the canoes! We've got to take her prisoner!" one girl yelled. "No, she's coming to shore," yelled another. Susan kept them guessing. She zigged toward the land one second, then zagged out into deeper water the next second. But all the while, she was leading the girls farther and farther down the beach, far away from the prison. Only Linda stayed near it, standing guard.

Molly scuttled out of the inlet like a crab, keeping an eye on Linda the whole time. She hid behind a bush while she caught her breath. But there was no time to waste. She pulled the lid off the can and sneaked quietly toward the prison. When Linda's back was turned, Molly dashed up behind her and yelled, "WORMS!" She dumped the stuff in the can on Linda's head. Spiders and stems went down the back of Linda's shirt. Sticks and bugs fell over her face. Worms were caught in her hair.

"ARRGH!" Linda howled. "Help!" She clawed at her hair, trying to pull the worms off. She jumped up and down wildly. Then she turned and saw Molly. "You?" she cried.

Molly froze. She was supposed to tag Linda and take her prisoner. She couldn't do it. This was Linda, her friend. She didn't look like the fierce Red Army guard anymore. She was plain old Linda, and

"Blue Army! Blue Army! You're free!" Molly yelled.
"Follow me!"

she looked like she was going to cry.

Molly ran away. She rushed toward her teammates who were prisoners. "Blue Army! Blue Army! You're free!" she yelled as she tagged them. "Follow me! Hurry up!"

With a great cheer, the Blue Army stampeded out of the prison. Linda didn't stop anyone. She was still pulling worms out of her hair. The Blue Army girls dragged their canoes into the lake, jumped into them, and paddled furiously, churning the water white. Some girls swam next to the canoes as their buddies paddled, and others had a leg up on the side of their canoes, trying to climb aboard.

When the Red Army girls saw what was happening, they ran crazily in all directions. Some headed up the hill to protect the flag. Some ran across the beach toward the prison. Some went to their canoes to try to chase the Blue Army. They were shouting, stumbling, and bumping into one another.

Susan paddled her canoe toward Molly, coming close to the shore. Molly swam as fast as she could to the canoe. "Get in! Get in!" cried Susan.

Molly pulled herself into the canoe. Carefully, Susan leaned way to the other side to balance Molly's weight. When she was safe in the canoe, Molly turned back to look at the beach.

Linda was standing all alone. Her hands hung down at her sides. She wasn't even trying to blow her whistle.

Molly made herself turn away. She picked up her paddle and followed the rest of the Blue Army back to camp. The war wasn't over yet, but Molly felt as if she had already lost something very important.

CHAPTER
FOUR

—

VICTORY AT SEA

 The Blue Army was rather quiet by the
time everyone got back to the boat-
house. "Here we are," sighed one girl.
"Right back where we started."

Molly looked at the downhearted girls. No one
knew what to do. "Where's Dorinda?" Molly asked.

A girl named Marie spoke up. "Dorinda wasn't
in the same prison with the rest of us. She was in a
special captain's prison. She didn't see you. I guess
she's still on the island."

"Serves her right," someone muttered.

"What'll we do now?" asked a tall girl named
Shirley. "Should we give up?"

"No!" said Molly. "We can win the war

without Dorinda."

"But who will be our leader?" asked Marie.

"I think it should be Molly," said Susan loyally. "She thought up the plan to free all of you. I didn't like it, but it worked. She can think up another plan to capture the flag and win the whole Color War. Can't you, Molly?"

"Yes," said Marie. "You be our captain, Molly."

Molly felt a little tickle of pride. But quickly she felt something else, too. *What if our army is captured again? Everyone will blame me. I will be the one who lost the war,* she thought. *I wonder if this is the way real leaders feel. I bet they felt this way before the D-Day invasion.* Molly thought about the newsreels she had seen of the D-Day invasion. The soldiers spilled out of the boats, ran across the beach, scrambled up the rocky cliffs along the shore. . . .

"Well?" Susan was asking her. "Do you have a plan?"

"I was just thinking," said Molly slowly. "Our Color War is sort of like the real war. We have to do what the Allies did on D-Day." Molly began to talk faster as she got excited. "The enemy—the Red

Army—knows we're going to try to land and invade their territory, just like the Nazis knew the Allies were going to land and invade France. The only thing they didn't know was exactly when and exactly where the Allies would land."

"Oh, for heaven's sake," said Shirley. "In our war the *when* is this afternoon and the *where* is the beach. There's no other time or place."

"We can't land on the beach again," said Molly, thinking out loud. "That's the mistake we made last time. The Red Army will be waiting for us there. We have to land someplace where they don't expect us."

"Like where?" Shirley asked.

Molly had an idea. She stepped over the sitting girls and went to the map. "Susan and I found a place when we fell out of— I mean, when we went to the island before," she said. "It's right . . . here!" Molly pointed to the map. She put her finger on the narrow landing place on Chocolate Drop Island. "It's a good place to land because the Red scout can't see it. It's hidden by rocky land on one side and trees on the other." Molly read the name off the map. "It's called Poison Point."

48

"But Molly," Susan piped up, "it's an awfully skinny place. Only one canoe can fit in it at a time."

"That's no good then," said Shirley. "We can't unload one canoe, then back it out, then unload the next. It would take too long. And how would we keep the empty canoes from floating away? We need a long beach or a long dock."

"Maybe we could build a dock on the island," said Marie.

"That's silly," said Shirley.

"No it isn't," said Molly. She thought of the D-Day newsreels again. "We can build a floating dock. That's what the Allies did when they landed in France."

Everyone looked blank.

"Don't you remember the newsreels we saw of D-Day?" Molly asked. "The Allies built a long, long  dock from the deep water all the way to the shore. Remember? They built it out of barges and boats. They could drive trucks off their big ships and onto their dock, and then all the way to land."

"I don't get it," said Susan. "We don't have any barges or anything. What can we use to build a dock?"

"Canoes," said Molly. "We'll use our canoes. We'll land one canoe at Poison Point, then we'll tie another canoe on to it. We'll tie all the canoes to one another end to end, in a long row. We can use our Camp Gowonagin ties. Then we'll walk from canoe to canoe, onto the island."

The girls murmured among themselves.

"That's crazy," someone said.

"Yes, but it might work," said Molly.

"I think we should try it," said Marie.

"All right, then!" Molly said. "Let's go!"

Susan was taking one last look at the map. "How come that place is called Poison Point?" she asked. "Are the rocks poison or something?"

But no one was there to answer Susan's question. Everyone was climbing back into the canoes. "Okay," shouted Molly. "I'll give each canoe a number. That will be your place in line. Susan will be in the first canoe and I will be in the last one." Molly pointed to each canoe. "One! Two!

Three! Four! Five! Six! Seven! Eight! Nine! Ten!
Ready? Head out!"

The Blue Army canoes followed Susan's canoe
across the lake. Molly noticed Susan seemed to be
paddling much straighter. Her canoe was a little
wobbly, but it didn't zig and zag as much as it used
to. When they got close to the island, Molly saw
the Red scout watching them. The scout turned and
ran back toward the beach.

Good, thought Molly. *They think we're silly
enough to land on the beach again. The Red Army will
be there waiting for us. They won't expect us to sneak
up on them from behind.*

Susan slipped her canoe into the landing place
at Poison Point. Canoe Number Two pulled up
behind her canoe, and Susan tied them together. In
no time, all ten canoes were tied end to end. The
girls kept low as they crawled from canoe to canoe
onto the island. Canoe Number Four almost turned
over, but luckily no one was in it at the time. Molly
was the last one to cross the rickety canoe dock
onto the land.

"Okay!" she said to the girls gathered on the
point. "Everyone from the first five canoes, go

The girls kept low as they crawled from canoe to canoe onto the island.

around to the beach. You'll have to swim a little, because there's an inlet just before you get to the prison. But you'll be able to sneak up on the Reds from behind the prison. Bring your Red Army prisoners back to camp in their own canoes. Everyone else will come up the hill with me to capture the flag. Let's go!"

No one moved.

"What's the matter?" asked Molly, exasperated.

"We found out why it's called Poison Point," said Susan. "This whole place is covered with poison ivy. No one wants to crawl through it."

Molly was determined. "We can't quit now," she said. "We have to . . . we have to . . .

Gowonagin! Gowonagin!

Go on again and try!"

The girls looked at each other uncomfortably.

Molly marched up and sat down smack in the middle of the poison ivy. She said,

"You can win! You can win!

Go on again and try!"

The girls giggled. Then Susan climbed up toward Molly. One by one every girl in the Blue

Army followed her. The girls climbed over the rocks carefully, trying to avoid the poison ivy leaves. One group headed toward the beach. The other group followed Molly up Chocolate Drop Hill.

At the top of the hill, Molly saw six Red Army girls guarding the flag. They were sitting in the sun eating their lunches, so they did not see Molly and the Blue Army sneaking up on them.

"One, two, three!" whispered Molly. She and her group fanned out, two Blue Army girls tagging each of the Red guards. Molly rushed to the very top of the hill. She pulled the flag out of the ground and waved it over her head.

"HURRAY!" the Blue Army girls cheered, jumping up and down and hugging one another. The Red guards were too stunned to do anything. Molly led everyone in a happy race back down the hill to the canoes. No one seemed to worry about poison ivy on the way down.

As Molly's group got back to Poison Point, the rest of the Blue Army came paddling around the island in the Red canoes they'd captured. In each canoe there was one Blue Army girl and two Red Army prisoners. When the Blue Army girls saw

Molly and the flag, they cheered, "Ya-hoo! We win!
Hurray, Blue Army! Hurray, Molly! Hurray! Hurray!"

Molly looked for Linda, but she couldn't find
her in the crowd. She did see Dorinda, who was
the only Blue Army girl who was not cheering.
Molly sat in the middle of a canoe, holding the flag
above her head. Across the lake they went. The
canoes followed a glittering path made by the
afternoon sun. Molly listened to the girls singing:

> "Raise the flag high,
>   Never say die,
>   While the red, white, and blue
>   flies above!"

Their voices were full of happiness. Molly was
happy, too. The Color War was over.

THE PINK ARMY

 Miss Butternut and the counselors
were waiting at the boathouse when
the girls got back to camp. Molly was
very glad to see the camp director's round, cheerful
face. She felt relieved when she put the flag in Miss
Butternut's hands.

Miss Butternut looked a little confused. "Uh,
congratulations, Blues," she said. "Good job,
Captain . . . Molly."

"Oh, I'm not the captain," said Molly. "Dorinda is really in charge."

"I see," said Miss Butternut. She looked over at
Dorinda, who was sulking. "Well," Miss Butternut
said briskly, "you can tell us the whole exciting

story later. But right now, I think everyone on both teams should report to the Dining Hall for a celebration. Ice cream cones for everyone!"

"Hurray! Ice cream!" shouted the girls. They ran up the hill to the Dining Hall.

As Molly was scooping ice cream into her cone, Miss Butternut said, "The counselors and I saw most of what happened, but we don't know *why* it happened that way. Perhaps you can tell us how it is that *you* ended up capturing the flag, Molly."

Molly didn't know where to begin. "Well . . ." she started.

Susan hurried forward. *"I'll* tell," she said. "Molly really saved the day. She did everything. You see, Dorinda was in prison. Actually, every-body in the Blue Army was in prison except Molly and me, because I tipped over our canoe. Then Molly thought up a plan to throw worms on Linda, because she was the prison guard, so we could free the Blue Army. We freed everybody, all except Dorinda. Then nobody knew what to do. So Molly thought up another plan. This time, we paddled over to Poison Point—"

"To where?" Miss Butternut interrupted. She

sounded worried.

"To Poison Point," Susan said. "We climbed—"

"WAIT!" cried Miss Butternut. She jumped up and stood on a chair. She blew a blast on her bugle and waved her other arm wildly. Everyone was so surprised, they were absolutely still. The Dining Hall had never been so quiet.

"Girls! Girls!" said Miss Butternut. "Stop! Before you get your cones, everyone who was at Poison Point go to the showers immediately. I want you to scrub, and I mean *scrub*, with strong soap. Then report to the camp nurse." Miss Butternut shook her head. "I'm afraid it's already too late. The whole bunch of you is going to have a walloping case of poison ivy!"

All the girls groaned.

Miss Butternut hurried the girls out of the Dining Hall. Even her hair looked frazzled. Her gray curls were standing out from her head like ruffled feathers.

Molly and Susan joined the sad parade. "Some victory celebration," sighed Susan. "Only the losers go to the party. The winners have to go to the nurse." Discouraged, Molly and Susan plodded up

the path to their tent to get their towels.

"Hey!" someone shouted. They turned around. It was Linda. "Wait up!" she said.

When Linda caught up to them, she was panting. "Here," she said. She gave each of them an ice cream cone.

"Gee, thanks!" said Susan. She was much cheerier. "It's nice of you to bring us ice cream. We thought you were mad at us about the worms."

Molly looked at Linda out of the corner of her eye.

"Well . . ." said Linda, a little sheepishly, "I

was mad. But then I figured you were mad at me
for blowing the whistle on you."

"We were surprised," said Molly. "We didn't
expect you to be so serious about the game."

Linda shrugged. "I guess I kind of wanted the
counselors to be proud of me," she said.

"Oh," said Molly.

"Well, if you ask me, it was a very mixed-up
day. No one acted normal," said Susan. She had a
dab of ice cream on her nose. "You were so serious
we had to throw worms at you. I spent the whole
day in a canoe. And Molly swam underwater, even
though no one asked her to."

Linda turned to Molly. "No kidding?" she
asked. "You swam underwater?"

"Yes," said Molly, "I did."

"Gosh," said Linda. "Then you *do* deserve to
win the Color War."

Molly grinned. "I don't think anybody really
won this war. I'm just glad it's over."

"Me too," said Linda.

"Me too," said Susan. "Now we can all have
fun together, like before."

"Yes," said Molly. "I don't want to be a Red or

a Blue or any other color ever again!"

But by the next morning, Molly, Susan, and almost everyone else at Camp Gowonagin *was* another color: POISON IVY PINK!

CALAMINE LOTION

CAMP
GOWONAGIN

Dear Dad,   July 6, 1944

Here I am carrying the flag in the Camp Gowonagin Fourth of July parade. Do you think my face looks funny? Well, it does. I have poison ivy. Just about everyone at camp does. How did we get it? Well Dad, that's a long story...

LOOKING
BACK
1944

A PEEK INTO
THE PAST

AMERICA OUTDOORS IN 1944

In 1944, it was hard for an American family to take a vacation together. Many families were separated by World War Two. Fathers were away fighting in the war. Mothers and some teenagers were working in factories, making war supplies. Even if families were together and had time for a vacation, travel was difficult.

From The Saturday Evening Post, August 24, 1940

Gasoline was rationed, so families couldn't take long car trips. And it was unpatriotic for them to use trains for unnecessary trips, because trains were needed to move soldiers and sailors across the country to ships that would take them to war.

Since families couldn't go on vacation together, many children took vacations alone at summer camp. In the 1940s, summer camps were like large parks in the woods, on lakes, or near the

Could this be you?

DON'T TRAVEL—UNLESS YOUR TRIP HELPS WIN THE WAR

Posters asked people not to drive unless they had to.

ocean. They were built as places for children to study nature and have fun outdoors. Campers lived in tents. They cooked over open fires. They had no electricity, so at night they used flashlights. They had only cold water and used outhouses rather than indoor plumbing. All of these things made campers like Molly feel as if they were living in the wilderness.

In fact, learning to live outdoors the way pioneers did was one of the most popular parts of camp life. Campers practiced starting a fire with only one match and built shelters using only a blanket and a few sticks. They studied pictures of wild animal tracks and learned which woodland plants were poisonous and which were safe to eat.

Campers learned outdoor survival skills.

Tents at a summer camp in the 1940s

Of course, children like Molly didn't really need to know any of these things because they weren't living in the wilderness. Cooks made most of their meals, and counselors were there to take care of them. They had tents and cabins to live in, and wild animals were nowhere close by. But learning wilderness skills was fun. And by learning them, campers learned to love

the outdoors. They also learned to respect the lives of native Americans and pioneers who had lived in the real wilderness.

In some ways, going to camp in the 1940s was like going to a wonderful school. Counselors planned every day so that campers would learn

Chores like gathering wood were part of the daily camp routine.

66

new things, and there was a special time for each camp activity. Campers had lessons in first aid, water safety, and nutrition. They made arts and crafts projects and learned horseback riding and swimming. They studied nature and took tests to see how well they could identify birds and trees, read a compass, and follow trail markings.

Children who went to camp during World War Two were taught to be patriotic, too. Every day began and ended with the Pledge of Allegiance and a flag ceremony. Some parts of camp life even reminded campers of

Familiar Trail Signs

These all mean "This is the way"

First sign means "Short distance this way"
Second sign means "Four miles to ____"
Third sign means "Long distance this way"

THE AMERICAN NATIONAL RED CROSS

Robyn Hansen

IS QUALIFIED AS A

Beginner in Swimming

HAVING PASSED THE REQUIRED TEST AT

Camp Tapawingo

Aafaed W. Criswell

ADMINISTRATOR FIRST AID, WATER SAFETY
AND ACCIDENT PREVENTION

July 18, 1944

Red Cross instructors taught campers to swim.

Quiet hour was for resting or reading.

what their fathers told them about life in the army or the navy. Campers lived together in groups like soldiers. Six or eight of them shared a tent or a cabin. They were responsible for keeping it clean and had daily inspections to see if their beds were made properly and their belongings were tidy. Camp outhouses were called *latrines* and meals were served in the *mess hall*. Both of these words came from military life.

During World War Two, while lucky children were off at summer camp, most adults were hard at work

Campers cleaned their tents for inspection.

in factories. They didn't take time to think about how factory smoke and soot were polluting the air. They were too busy thinking about what war materials were being made inside factories. But organizations like the Girl Scouts, Boy Scouts, and the Red Cross, which ran many summer camps, remembered that it was impor-tant to teach children how to live comfort-ably and safely outdoors. And the campers they taught grew up to be adults who cared about protecting the environ-ment so that people like you can enjoy camping for a few weeks each summer, too.

Badges like these rewarded Girl Scout campers who learned outdoor skills.

THE AMERICAN GIRLS COLLECTION®

FELICITY   KIRSTEN®   ADDY   SAMANTHA   MOLLY

There are more books in The American Girls Collection. They're filled with the adventures that five lively American girls lived long ago.

The books are the heart of The American Girls Collection, but they are only the beginning. There are also lovable dolls that have beautiful clothes and lots of wonderful accessories. They make these stories of the past come alive today for American girls like you.

To learn about The American Girls Collection, fill out this postcard and mail it to Pleasant Company, or call **1-800-845-0005.** We will send you a catalogue about all the books, dolls, dresses, and other delights in The American Girls Collection.

I'm an American girl who loves to get mail. Please send me a catalogue of The American Girls Collection®:

My name is _____

My address is _____

City _____ State _____ Zip_____

Parent's signature _____

3802

And send a catalogue to my friend:

My friend's name is _____

Address _____

City_____ State _____ Zip_____

1229

If the postcard has already been removed from this book and you would like to receive a Pleasant Company catalogue, please send your full name and address to:

PLEASANT COMPANY
P.O. Box 620497
Middleton, WI 53562-9940
or, call our toll-free number
1-800-845-0005

BUSINESS REPLY MAIL
First Class Mail   Permit No. 1137   Middleton, WI USA

POSTAGE WILL BE PAID BY ADDRESSEE

PLEASANT COMPANY
P.O. Box 620497
Middleton, WI 53562-9940